I Hum Every Day

To Pam, my wife,
who taught me to sit quietly and listen to small sounds.

July 3, 2020

©2023
ISBN# 978-1-7923-9351-8

Illustrations copyright William P. Hamilton ©2023

I Hum Every Day

Matt Farmer

Matt Farmer

Illustrated by
Wil Hamilton

Wil Hamilton

Acknowledgments

My heartfelt thanks to Jac Bird and Wil Hamilton for their support and suggestions throughout the story development, to Richard Weaver for his selfless work in editing, and in blending the text and the illustrations into an actual book; and to my wife, Pam, for her persistent encouragement throughout the process. The efforts of family and friends are the real story here.

Birth

It seemed to me like I laid in the warm wet dark forever. Then one day a small crack appeared in the dark. This so excited me that I began pecking and pushing at the crack. Soon the whole dark roof of my world cracked wide open and I fell right out into my mother's nest. I wasn't alone. A smooth hard egg was next to me and I could hear movement inside it.

As my eyes got used to the light, I could make out my mother standing on the edge of the nest looking down at me with gentle eyes. Next thing I knew she stretched her wings out from her sides, and they started to make a humming sound. She rose straight up in the air and disappeared through the leaves and branches of the tree where we live.

Mother was soon back. In her long beak she had a bug rolled up in nectar. This treasure she offered to me, and she called me "Hummer." Something made me take the bug and swallow it down. Mm-mm, good. Really good!

The next day I started to feel movement in the egg next to me. Shortly thereafter I noticed a small crack. I could see a little beak pecking away at the crack from the inside. Soon the whole top of the egg cracked wide open and this scrawny ugly little bird fell right out into the nest.

2

I did what I could to make the ugly little thing as welcome and comfortable as possible. About all I could do was move over and use my beak to help it get upright. Once we had this sorted, Mom took off again on her humming wings.

Soon she was right back with another bug rolled in nectar in her beak. This time she offered her treasure to my nest mate and called her "Amelia." Amelia took the bug and swallowed it down without so much as a "by your leave" to me.

I checked and discovered I had wings just like my mother's. I made up my mind to give that "humming" a try the first chance I got. I was very interested in where Mother went to get bugs and nectar.

Learning to Fly

My chance to try humming came just two weeks later. By then I was old enough to stand up in the nest and stretch out my wings. No matter how hard I tried to flap them, they wouldn't hum. All Amelia said to me was, "Humph! As if."

Mother decided it was time to explain to me how and why hummingbird wings hum. "Most birds have fixed-shape wings," she began. "They drive through the air forward by flapping their wings down and then gliding as the wings come back up for another down stroke. Their wing cycle is a slow flap-glide, flap-glide; much like children sometimes flap their arms to pretend to fly. Of course young humans don't have weight saving hollow bones or big wing muscles, so they can't actually fly. We hummingbirds, on the other hand, can drive our wings both down and forward and up and back in a curve that is so fast our wings vibrate and hum."

"OK, Hummer, hold out your wings. You have to find the right up and back angle to start with. That looks good. Now swing, don't flap, your wings forward and a little down. Feel the air rush over your wings? When the wings have gone about as far forward as they can, make a smooth half-circle to turn the wings over and swing them back to where they started. Swing forward again like you are trying to clap them together. Repeat the cycle faster and faster. When you do it correctly, you will soon feel your wings begin to vibrate and then hear them "hum." This will happen when you hit about 60 wing beats per second. That is very fast, Hummer. Only hummingbirds can do it, and then only by making the effort to learn how."

Whew! That was a lot for a bird brain to keep track of. Fortunately I didn't have to. The whole cycle just came naturally for me.

I got to work practicing humming every day. After some long days of serious effort I heard a dull hum come from my wings. I practiced harder and longer. To keep me going Mother kept stuffing bugs rolled in nectar down my throat. Amelia got nectar-bugs too even though she was too young and scrawny to practice humming. Everyone should have a mother like mine.

Finally, I heard a strong regular hum from my wings and I was very happy. Mother heard the hum too. She said it was time to talk about flying. Amelia heard the humming and just said, "Well, you got the right name anyway."

True to her word, as she always was, Mother told me about flying the very next day. She said, "Humming takes muscle power and wing speed. Flying, however, takes finesse and fine wing shape control. Remember that, Hummer, and you can become a great flyer."

I thought I could too, if only I knew what "finesse" meant.

"To fly, you make continuous changes to your wing speed and shape based on what you feel in the air," she added. Which turns out to be what finesse means in flying.

"Now, Hummer, watch me." With that, Mother shot straight up about five feet and came to an abrupt stop in mid-air. She hung there on humming wings and yelled down, "Hummer, what did you see me do to fly?"

"Nothing Ma. I didn't see nothing."

"Anything. You didn't see anything," Mom corrected automatically.

"Anything," Amelia repeated with a snicker.

"You didn't see anything because you can't see "lift," the invisible force that pushes up on your wings when they're humming. In fact, everything that flies uses lift to stay in the air: birds, bugs, bats, airplanes, etc.

As you speed up your wings, pushing back a little against the increasing lift on your wings raises you right up into the air. Now you can fly forward or backward or sideways. You can even fly upside down. No other bird can do that."

"A hummingbird's wing cycle creates lift on both the forward and the backward stroke," she continued, "Get your wing shape wrong and your wings will "stall." Do that and you will lose your lift and go out of control, falling out of the sky."

Flying suddenly made sense to me. So, I got a good hum going and focused on feeling the lift coming from my humming wings. It was easy from there on. I shot up out of the nest and was soon hanging in the air right next to my mother. She looked over at me with shining-happy eyes. All she said was, "Follow me."

"Follow me"

Stunts

With that, she flew up through the branches and leaves of our home tree, with me right on her tail. As we flew out of our tree I took a good look at the world around us. Beautiful. Actually, spectacular!

There were lots and lots of green trees, some much bigger, others much smaller, than our home tree. There were big green fields. In and around the fields were many bright colored spots. These colored spots were, for some reason, of immediate and great interest to me. Evidently mother was as interested in the colored spots as I was.

The next thing I knew, we were diving straight down toward a particularly brightly colored corner of a field. Wow, really fun and really exciting! Going down was a lot easier than going up and soon we were going so fast I began to worry about stopping.

No worries though. Mother knew what to do. She told me to come up and fly beside her. When I got there, she sped up the dive. So did I. This was disconcerting as we were side by side going straight down and very fast. Then Mother did something I didn't expect. She threw her head back hard, stood straight up in flight and used her humming wings to stop in midair. This so surprised me that I shot right by her. Now I was really concerned. At what seemed to me like the last second, I threw my head back hard, stood up in flight, and hummed so hard and fast, I thought I might pull a wing off.

Instead I came to a screeching halt right next to one of those bright colored spots. Up close what had looked like a colored spot from up high, looked suspiciously like a flower. My suspicion was confirmed a second later when Mother cruised right by me and casually stuck her beak into the center of a flower. When she pulled back a couple of seconds later, I thought I saw her lick some nectar off her beak. Then she turned toward me and said, "You try it, Hummer."

I did. The mystery of where Mother got nectar was solved. That's when I noticed all the bugs on and in the air around the flowers. Another mystery solved. I immediately started pestering Mother about the best way to catch bugs. Mother had no time for bug catching philosophy; she just started racing from flower to flower without another word.

When she was done, she said she had one more thing to show me and took off in the direction of our home tree. When we got there, she flew around to what would be our front yard (if we had yards). There she pulled up to this weird-looking device with little hummingbird perches at intervals all the way around it. Mother took a perch and soon had her beak sticking in the little hole conveniently placed right in front of the perch. Who placed that little hole there and what was in it were complete mysteries to me.

I got a clue what might be in the hole when mother pulled her beak out, and I thought I saw the tell-tale glint of nectar on her beak. "Here, Hummer, take my perch," she said, rising up to a nearby bare branch to watch.

I hummed right over, took the perch, and stuck my little beak in the hole. Nectar, sweet nectar! And it never ran out. All you can eat nectar right in my front yard! "Better and better," that's what I thought. I wanted to fly right up to her branch and ask mother, "What's next?"
But I didn't.

Instead I got my hum going and started climbing to see what the world looked like from even higher than Mom had taken me. Just a few seconds later when I looked down at our big home tree, it looked like a bush. "Altitude," Mother had called it. Whatever it's called, I liked it. Altitude could be turned into speed.

I tipped right over, pointed straight down at the home tree and poured on the speed. This time I knew what to expect. When I started seeing the ground come up really fast I didn't throw my head back and stand straight-up in flight. Instead I just eased my head up and pulled out level to the ground going 60 miles an hour.

Swooop! I shot by the home tree, scattering the sparrows at the seed-feeder as I pulled up hard and dodged right to miss a droopy old cedar tree. As soon as I slowed down, Mom caught up with me. All she said was, "Hummer, do that sort of flying out in the open field, not in the front yard."

Like I said — better and better. I zipped right down to the field and started climbing for altitude. When I got there, I did a lazy back loop and let it fall through into another head down screaming-fast dive. "Big finish," I thought as the speed started to plaster my feathers to my body, "What I need is a big finish."

I decided to pull out of the dive inverted (back to earth) instead of the usual belly down position. I tried this first up high above the field-and a good thing too. Instead of an inverted pull-out what I did was something called a "high-speed stall." I don't know what exactly that is, but what I saw when I did it was left wing-right wing-left wing-right wing-left wing-right wing-tail-sky-tail-sky-ground-wing-wing-sky-ground-sky. Talk about disconcerting! This swirling, twirling out of control display ended, once I stopped tumbling, with a casual hover in among the flowers (which is where I just happened to end up).

13

I took a quick look around to see if anyone was watching and headed for home. Mother said, "Well—nice recovery. It looked to me like you might need a little work on your inverted wing shape."

Amelia said sarcastically, "Yeah, nice recovery. They should change your name to Nice Recovery. That's all I ever see you do."

I headed back to the field and started climbing again. Lazy back loop falling into a screaming dive and then another inverted pull-out, this time concentrating on wing shape. I shot out across the field upside down at 60 miles an hour. Now all I needed for my big finish was to get the pull-out right down on the deck (near the ground.) Beautiful! When I got back to the nest, Amelia had to say, "Hey, Nice Recovery, I see you finally learned something. That was cool!"

Meanwhile the hummingbird feeder in the front yard was calling me home. Mother told me a nice human lady kept the feeder full of nectar just for us hummingbirds. "But," Mother warned, "Don't start thinking all humans are friends. Some are vicious little creeps who will hurt other living things."

I didn't know any humans like that so I didn't worry about it. I did, however, see an adult human use a big machine to cut down and kill all the flowers and everything else in the field next to the road. Now the field has no food or safe places so I have to avoid it.

Two days later, Amelia tried her first flight with Mother. She did well but I could tell she wasn't the daredevil experimenting type. She took to hanging around the feeder with the other girl hummingbirds. We would meet at the nest each night and talk about the day's activities but our interests diverged: she liked to explore nest building and feeding sources, but, for me, I was into speed and power, the more the better. Soon the nest wasn't big enough for both of us and we began sleeping perched on nearby branches just like Mom did.

Migration

Some mornings now the nectar in the feeder was too thick and cold to drink. The flowers were all but gone and it was getting hard to find enough to eat. That meant less flying and more hanging around the home tree. Mother said winter was coming. She had a big adult explanation involving the Earth tilting away from the sun, causing shorter days and colder temperatures.

Whatever.

Winter meant all hummingbirds, and many other birds too, had to fly south where it was warmer and there would be more bugs and flowers for food. Next year when the Earth tilted back, we would all return to what Mother called our breeding (whatever that is?) grounds.

"Hummingbirds," mother told me, "don't 'flock-up' like other birds to make the trip south. Instead each hummingbird flies down there alone."

"Fly low and look for flowers and bugs the whole way," she advised.

I had a lot of questions about how, exactly, this might work. Mother told me not to worry. How to do it was in something called my genes. Because of these genes, I'd know what to do.

"OK, Mom. Solo to South America. No sweat. Uh, which way is South?"

Mom offered the hint that the sun rose in the east and set in the west. I knew that, but I couldn't see how that helped. Mother flew down to the front yard and scratched a big cross in the dirt with her beak. At the top of the cross, she wrote "N" for north, at the bottom "S" for south. At the right end of the center, she wrote "E " for east and at the left "W" for west.

Approximate Range Map for Black Chinned Hummingbirds

Canada

United States

Breeding resident
(yellow)

Migratory visitor
(green)

Year Round
Resident
(purple)

Mexico

Nonbreeding Resident
(blue)

16

"Now, Hummer, where does the sun go down?"

"Easy one, Mom. Right over there," I said, pointing with my beak.

"OK, good. Now turn to point at that place with your right wing. Which way is your beak pointing now?"

I looked down at her cross in the dirt and said "South, Ma. South."

"Clever boy," she said. But I didn't feel very clever. I wondered how, even if I could fly south every day, I'd know when I got there.

Mother said: "Don't worry. Just fly south as far as you can and then find a place with lots of flowers and bugs. Hang out there until it starts to get colder and the days get shorter again. When that happens, it will be starting to get warmer here and it will be time to return for the breeding season."

"OK, Mom, I can do that. But what is a "breeding season?"

"Well, do you remember how I would give you and Amelia bugs rolled in nectar when you were little baby hatchlings?"

"Sure, Mom. We were too little to know what to eat, let alone where to find it."

"That's right, Hummer. I had to get food for you and Amelia. Every other mother hummingbird had to get food for her babies, too. That's why hummingbird babies hatch in the spring when there are a lot of flowers and bugs. That makes spring the breeding season for hummingbirds and lots of other birds too. We, and all other living things, are part of a natural cycle that has evolved over millions and millions of years." It felt good to be part of a natural cycle, and I was ready to fly south when the time came.

The time came about a week later after a killing frost. A killing frost is when it gets so cold at night that the water in plant leaves freezes. Freezing kills the leaves and then the plants, including most flowers. That means less food for hummingbirds, and it is time to fly south. First Mother took off and a day later, so did Amelia. I decided to leave after two more days of filling up at the hummingbird feeder.

Flying south turned out to be very lonely and sometimes even frightening, being just one tiny bird all alone in the great big world. It was also boring because there was no time or extra energy for climbing up high to do dives and stunts. I just cruised south all day every day trying to save energy and looking for that next bug or flower I needed to keep going. Not really fun but it is part of being a hummingbird, so that's what I did.

Hawk Attack

The very next day, as I was crossing a mountain ridge, I got more "fun" than I'd bargained for. I had no sooner crossed the ridge and started down the grassy other side when I saw a bird shadow right below me. Puzzled because the shadow obviously wasn't mine, I rolled inverted and found myself looking up at the huge bright yellow talons of a hooked-beak diving hawk.

I knew instinctively I couldn't outrun this bird. I pulled up hard and started racing full speed straight up right at the diving hawk. This so surprised the hawk that I was able to dodge right past her.

Once past her, I looked back down and was gratified to see the hawk roll inverted to follow my passing. I knew only hummingbirds can fly upside down and, sure enough, the hawk lost all her air speed and fell, spinning slowly back toward earth for a few seconds before she managed to struggle back upright. Meanwhile I continued climbing as fast as I could go, giving me the advantage of altitude. Once I had that advantage, I rolled back down, poured on the speed and aimed right at the struggling hawk. To add insult to injury, I gave the hawk a good peck in the back of the head as I whizzed by.

As soon as I was past the hawk, I aimed directly at the side of the ridge below us. This deprived the hawk of any gliding advantage, shortened the distance to the ground and steepened our descent angle. The hawk made a couple of half-hearted swipes at me with her talons as I went by. She rolled vertical above me, and the chase was on. I really poured on more speed straight down, and I kept pouring it on until I was closer to the ground and going faster than I had ever gone before. The hawk was right there behind me. At the very last possible second I did an inverted pull-out. This shocked the hawk who thought she had me trapped — and she would have if not for the inverted pull-out. Unable to fly inverted, the hawk had no choice but to throw one wing up, the other wing down and try a very steep and very high-speed 180 degree turn.

19

It was incredible to see a large bird attempt such a maneuver. For just a second I worried she might actually make it. Then I was treated to the wildest high-speed stall ever imagined.

The hawk looked like a large feather duster doing cartwheels down the hill. As I started climbing back up the ridge to resume my trip south, the hawk was laying upside-down in a small pile of her own feathers. If she hadn't been trying to catch and eat me, I might have felt sorry for her. I could still well remember my first high-speed stall, which was nothing compared to the hawk's.

As I flew upward along the highest rocky part of the ridge, I noticed a large, somewhat haphazard nest on a ledge. Inside were two gawky (and 'hawky') little birds covered in white pin feathers. As I crested the ridge, I saw the hawk far below collect herself and struggle into the air. She swung around and began gliding away down the slope, on the hunt for easier food.

I kept heading south for a few more days until, just like Mother said, there were a lot of bugs and flowers. There I settled down to wait for breeding season.

When the time came to head back north, I was anxious to get back to my home tree and to see my mother again, although I didn't really know if seeing my mother again was part of the hummingbird natural cycle or not. It turns out, not.

All I had to guide me from now on was whatever was in those genes Mother told me about. Evidently there was a lot in there because, as soon as I got back up north, I somehow knew to start looking for a good territory with lots of flowers and even a feeder if possible.

Breeding Season

Fortunately for me, my navigation skills were excellent, and after several days of flying north, I recognized a particularly brightly colored corner of a field. The hummingbird feeder I fed from last year was still present and filled with nectar. The home tree, however, was gone. Where it went, I have no idea. All that is there now is a stump. I figure its disappearance must be part of a natural cycle, just like me.

This looked like a good territory to me. I settled in to claim it. Claiming turned out to mean sitting on a high perch all day and running off any male hummingbirds that came into my territory. Running off usually just meant chasing them away and that's when my hard-won flying skills really paid off.

Flying skills paid off even more when the next phase of breeding season arrived. A week or so after I claimed my territory, female hummingbirds began to show up. Something (probably my genes) told me not to chase away these pretty, shiny green birds. Instead the genes told me to start showing off my flying skills, including death dives with inverted pull-outs just inches off the ground.

Inverted pull-outs created considerable stir among the girls. They flocked around and talked and giggled. I didn't pay them much mind until one day a girl named "Lianne" hummed over and started asking about inverted flight. I could tell, just from the tone of her hum, that she too was a natural flyer. She clearly "got" flying.

I explained, "Inverted flight is just using the backstroke of your hum instead of the forward stroke as your primary means of lift."

"Be careful, though, to flatten your wing shape if you're going fast inverted, like coming out of a dive," I continued, "If you don't, the air will separate from your wings and you will lose your lift and your control."

With that, I said, "Follow me."

We hummed off, side by side across the field to where I started a full speed climb. At the top of the climb, I rolled inverted, and there she was, flying inverted right beside me. Now that's exciting! I didn't really know what to do, so I dropped into a screaming fast dive figuring we'd see what would happen when I pulled out inverted. What happened was she cruised right by me inverted, kicking her little feet as she went. I was beside myself; excited, happy and very confused. Fortunately my genes came to my rescue again and instead of saying something stupid, I just asked her what she was doing.

"Dancing," she said.

I caught up with her, rolled back inverted right beside her and started kicking my feet too. Lianne pulled ahead and the next thing I knew, we were flying through the leaves and branches of a huge old tree right behind the flower patch in the corner of the field. We stopped at a small nest she had built in the crook of a high branch. Lianne dropped right down in the nest. She invited me to join her which I did. There we were, beak to beak and belly to belly in a little nest high in a big tree right near where my mother first taught me to fly the year before. I didn't really understand it but, just like that, breeding was over.

Lianne was soon very busy becoming a mother herself. In a few days she laid her first egg and a second one a day later. I continued my summer job of defending food sources for the babies and her, and when autumn arrived, I fattened up at the feeder and headed south again.

I fly south every winter and return for breeding season every spring. A hummingbird's natural cycle is a good one, and I am happy. Still, I never again had a breeding season like the one I had with Lianne, which is why I sometimes wish hummingbirds mated for life. But they don't.

© Hamilton 2021

Penny

One day, as I was hanging around the feeder, the nice lady who keeps it full came out to fill the feeder and with her was a little girl who looked just like her. The little girl sat down and spoke directly to me, politely calling me "Mr. Hummingbird." This was so adorable, I wished there was some way for me to communicate with this human.

My hummingbird voice was obviously not going to work but as I listened closely to her gentle voice, I began to think I might have enough control over the sound of my humming wings that I could mimic human speech with them. Of course, the frequency of human speech was much too low for me to fly and mimic human speech at the same time. I was sitting comfortably on a perch at the feeder so I got my wings humming, dropped their pitch down to the range of human speech and tried. "Hello, what's your name?" Without so much as a flinch, she told me, "Penny."

I now had a human friend, which was really different but really fun. One morning, sometime later, Penny told me she had to walk to school because she is old enough now.

"How do you feel about that?" I asked her, thinking I heard some strain in her voice.

"Well," she said, "I'm a little nervous about it to tell you the truth. I don't want to get lost."

"Maybe I could fly along with you and keep an eye on you from above."

"Oh, could you?", she gushed.

"I can and I will." I told her. "Don't worry. I know right where your school is."

Once we got to school I had a chance to say "Hi" to some of the other kids I had seen from around the neighborhood. Only those who could sit still and listen to the little sounds around them could hear me. For some reason, every human I talk to seems a little startled. Is it me or are humans just jumpy?

Much as I enjoyed talking with my new human friends, winter was coming back. I started the journey south again, continuing my natural cycle.

In time, Penny grew up and went off to something called college. When I saw her again some years later, she had with her a little girl that looked just like her. Evidently hummingbirds aren't the only ones with genes and a natural cycle. When I asked Penny's little girl her name, she said, "My name is Megan. You must be Hummer. Mother told me about her hummingbird friend, but I thought you might be imaginary."

Well, I'm not imaginary, and maybe if you're one of the humans who can sit quietly and listen to little sounds around you, we can meet someday. I know I'd like that. Maybe you would too.

The End

What Hummingbirds Eat

*Hummingbirds' main food source is nectar from flowers,
especially tube-shaped flowers, with the occasional small bug or spider.
Hummingbird feeders can supplement flowers, with sugar water only.
Mix a ratio of one part sugar to four parts water (no coloring!).
The feeder must be kept free of mold and fungi which can actually kill
the hummingbirds.
Excellent websites about hummingbirds and feeding them include
The Audubon Society and Cornell University's All About Birds.*

Did you see some Hummingbirds?

_____

_____

_____

_____

_____

_____

_____

_____

_____

_____

_____

_____

_____

_____

_____

_____

_____

_____

Made in the USA
Monee, IL
23 June 2023